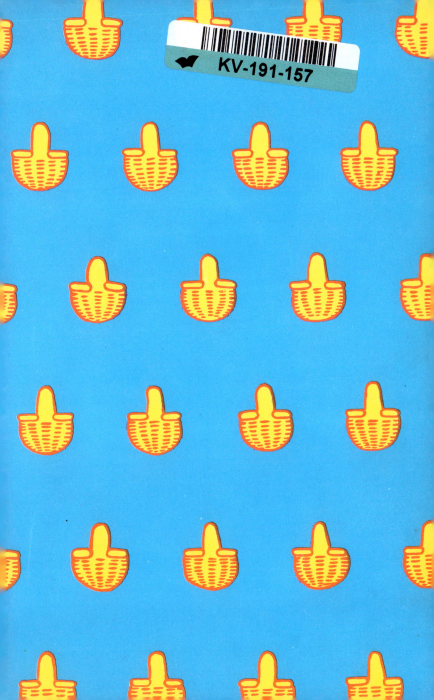

NOTE TO PARENTS

This well known fairytale has been specially written and adapted for 'first readers', that is, for children who are just beginning to read by themselves. However, if your child is not yet able to read, then why not read this story aloud to him or her, pointing to the words and talking about the pictures? There is a word list at the back of the book which identifies difficult words and explains their meaning in the context of the story.

Little Red Riding Hood

retold by Clare Caddock
illustrated by Gill Guile

Copyright © 1990 by World International Publishing Limited.
All rights reserved.
Published in Great Britain by World International Publishing Limited,
An Egmont Company, Egmont House,
P.O. Box 111, Great Ducie Street,
Manchester M60 3BL.
Printed in DDR.
ISBN 0 7235 4498 0

A CIP catalogue record for this book is available from the British Library

Once there was a little girl.
She wore a bright red cape.
The cape had a hood, so everyone
called her Red Riding Hood.

One day her mother called to her.
"I've made a basket of food.
Will you take it to Grandma?"
Red Riding Hood said she would.
She promised not to talk to
any strangers on the way.

Red Riding Hood set off.
The path went through a forest.
The birds were singing and all
the little animals were playing.
She stopped to pick some flowers.

Suddenly a wolf appeared.
"Where are you going?" he asked.
"I'm taking this basket of food
to Grandma's," Red Riding Hood said.
The wolf said goodbye and went away.

Red Riding Hood picked some
more flowers for Grandma.
It was a lovely day.
She skipped along in the sunshine.
She would soon be at Grandma's.

The wolf had a nasty plan.
He knew where Grandma lived.
He raced through the woods.
He wanted to get to Grandma's
before Red Riding Hood.

The wolf saw Grandma's house.
It was just over the hill.
A little rabbit saw the wolf.
It ran away quickly.
But the wolf didn't have time
to chase rabbits.

The wolf hurried to the house.
He knocked on the door.
Grandma opened it.
The wolf ran inside.
He nearly knocked Grandma over.

"You naughty wolf!" cried Grandma.
"Be quiet," growled the wolf.
"Bring me some of your clothes."
Grandma did as she was told.
Then the wolf tied her up.
He shut Grandma in a cupboard.

The wolf put on Grandma's clothes.
Then he put on her glasses.
"I look just like Grandma," he said.
"Now I'll get into Grandma's bed."

Meanwhile, Red Riding Hood had
nearly reached Grandma's house.
But she didn't know where the
wolf was.

Red Riding Hood's basket was
beginning to feel very heavy.
She got to Grandma's door.
But it was already open.
I'll surprise Grandma, she thought.
Red Riding Hood tip-toed in.

The wolf was waiting for her.
"Hello, Grandma,"
said Red Riding Hood.
The wolf made his voice sound
just like Grandma's.
"Hello, dear," he said.
"What a nice surprise this is."

"I've brought you some food,"
said Red Riding Hood.
She put the basket on the bed.
Then she stared at the wolf.

Grandma's ears were sticking out
of her nightcap!
"Oh, Grandma," said Red Riding Hood.
"What big ears you have!"

The wolf smiled.
"All the better to hear you
with, my dear," he said.
Then he stared at Red Riding Hood.

Grandma's eyes looked very strange
through her glasses.
"Oh, Grandma," said Red Riding Hood.
"What big eyes you have!"

The wolf smiled.
"All the better to see you
with, my dear," he said.
Then he licked his lips.

Grandma's teeth looked very sharp
as she licked them.
"Oh, Grandma!" cried Red Riding Hood.
"What big teeth you have!"

The wolf was very hungry now.
"All the better to eat you
with, my dear," he roared.
And he leapt out of bed.
Red Riding Hood was very frightened.
She screamed and screamed.

A goose was flying past.
It heard the little girl's screams.
It flew away to get help.
A woodman was working nearby.
When he heard what was happening
he ran to Grandma's house.

He was still carrying his axe.
When the wolf saw the axe
he fainted with fright.
Red Riding Hood pointed to
the small cupboard.
Grandma was kicking at the door.

They unlocked the cupboard and
untied Grandma.
Grandma gave Red Riding Hood a
great big hug.
"Thank you for saving our lives,"
she said to the woodman.

"Let's have a picnic," said Red
Riding Hood.
"We can share all the food
I brought for Grandma."
All the forest animals came too.
They were very happy.
The big, bad wolf would never
bother them again.

New words

Did you see lots of new words in the
story? Here is a list of some hard words
from the story, and what they mean.

bother
they would not have to worry
about the wolf again

cape
a coat with no sleeves

faint
the wolf fell to the ground

frightened
Red Riding Hood was scared

growled
the wolf made a growly noise
when he talked

hurried
went very quickly

meanwhile
whilst something else was happening